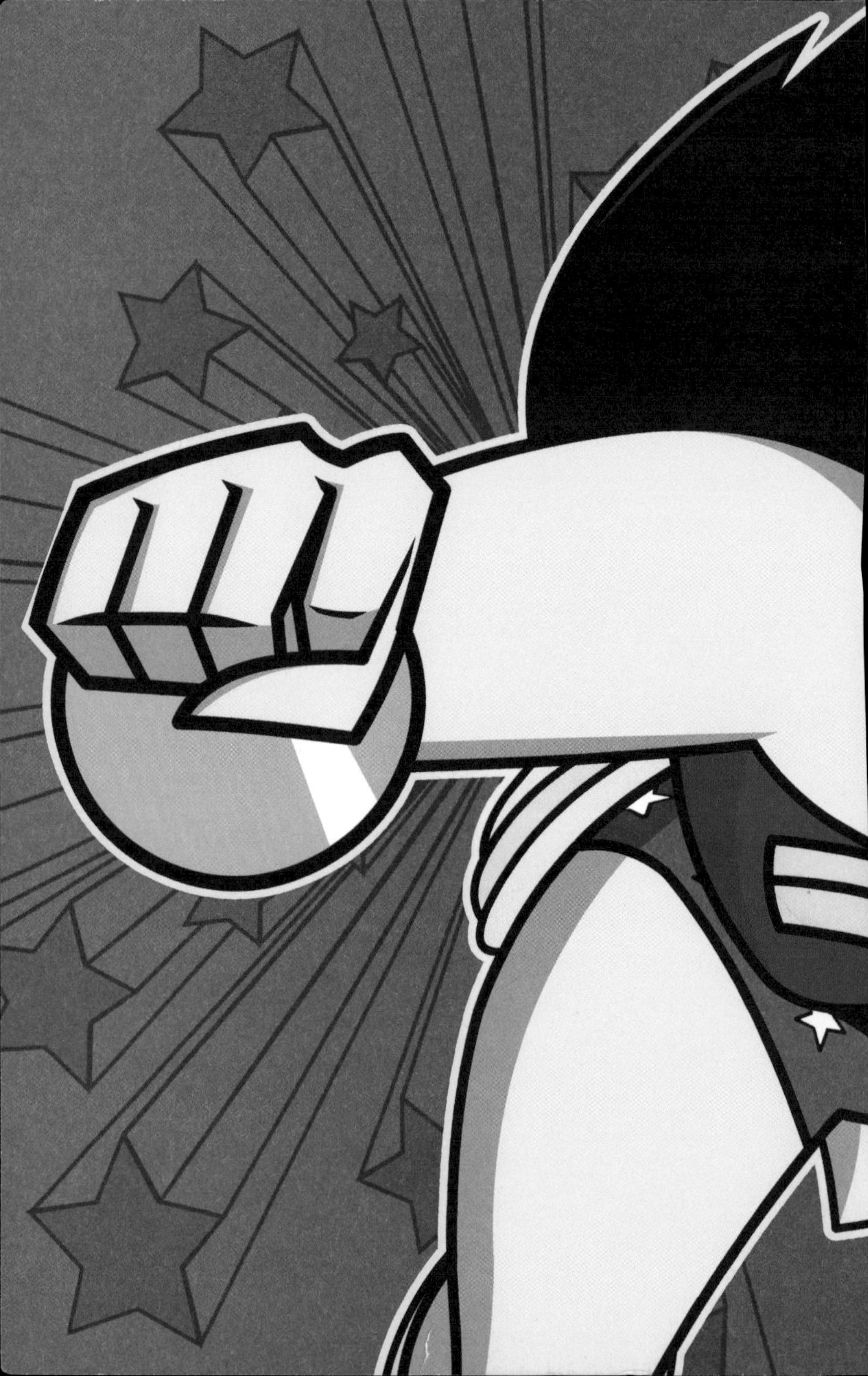

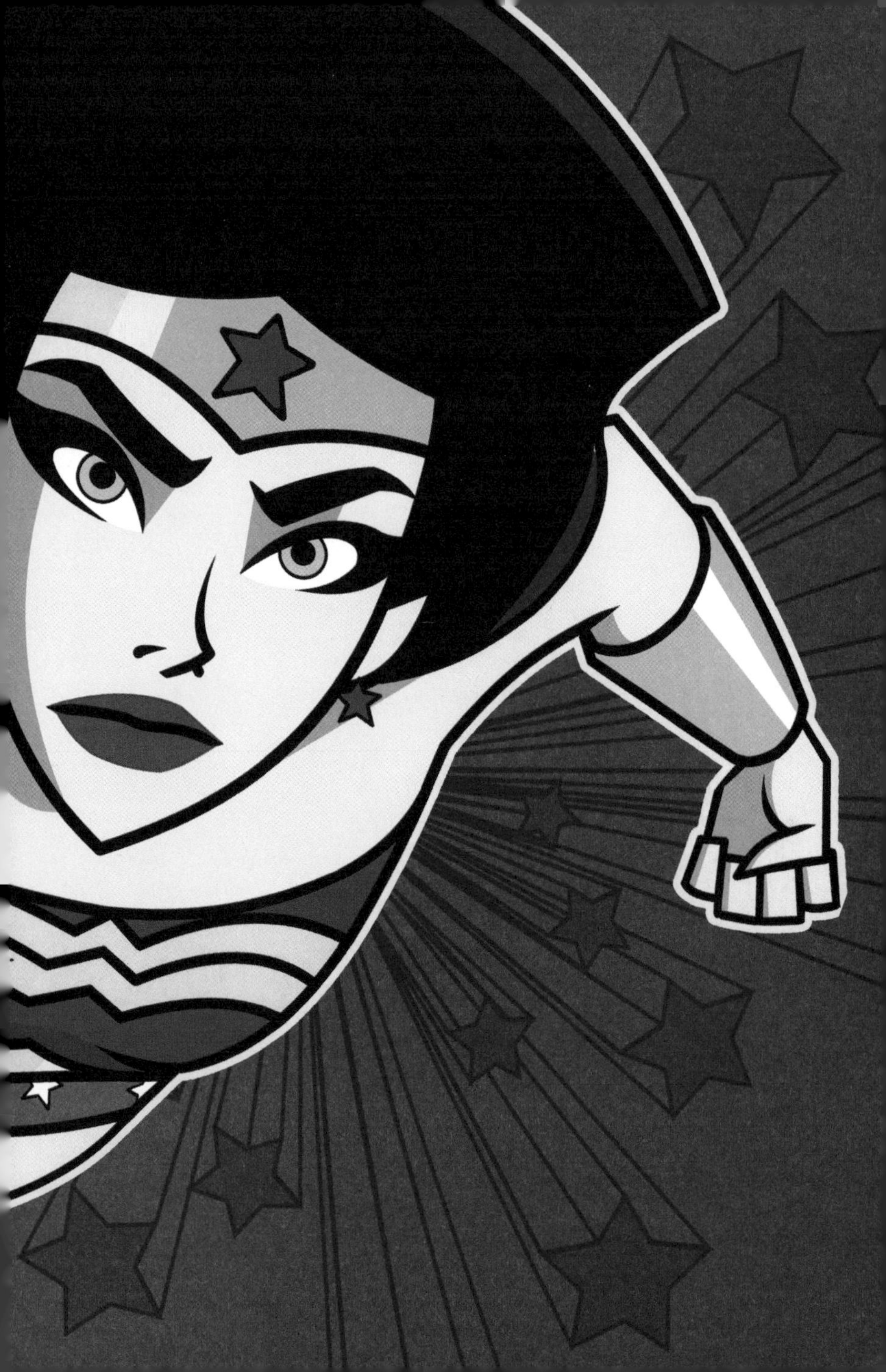

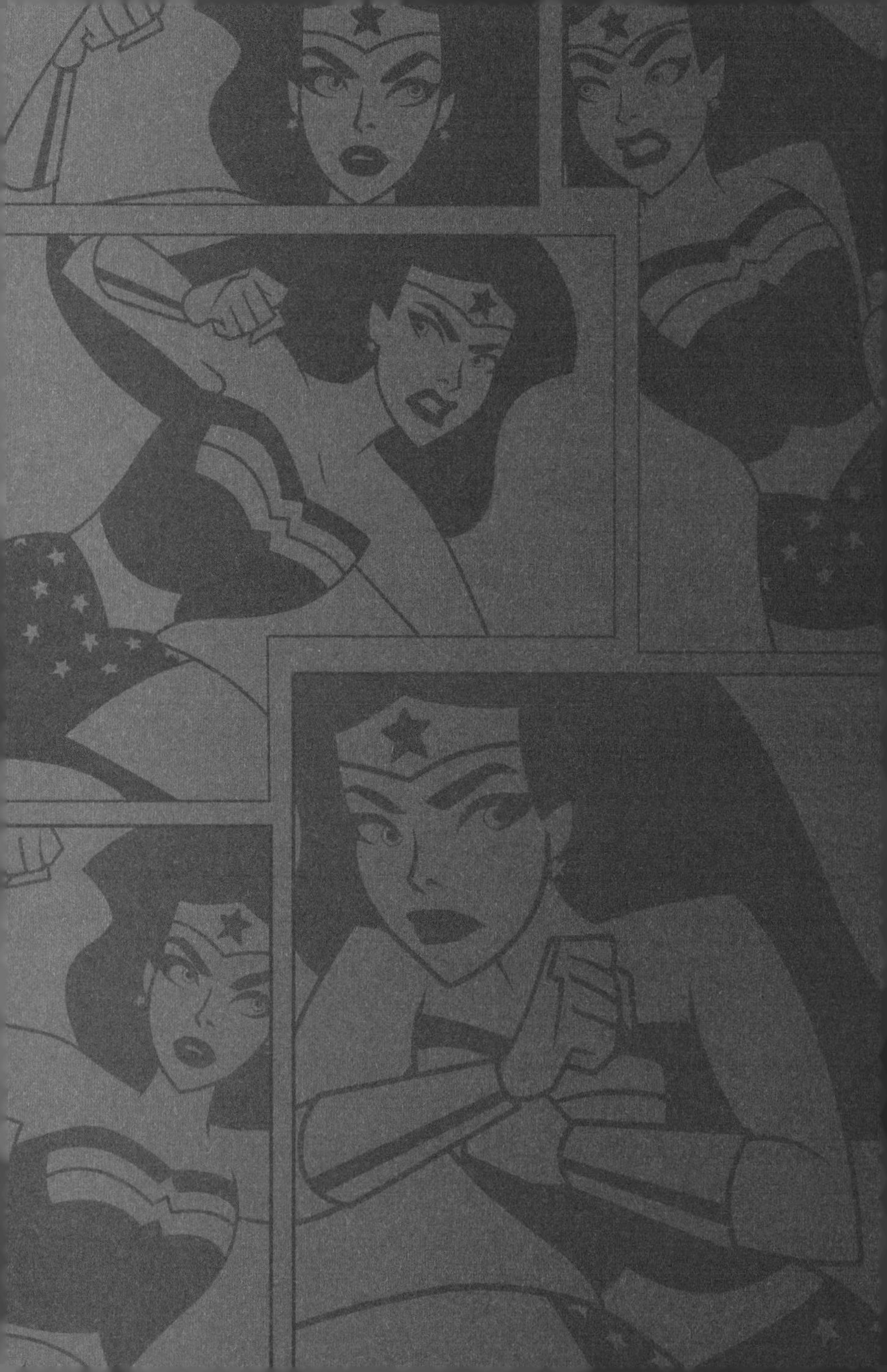

SUPER DC HEROES

WONDER WOMAN

TRIAL OF THE AMAZONS

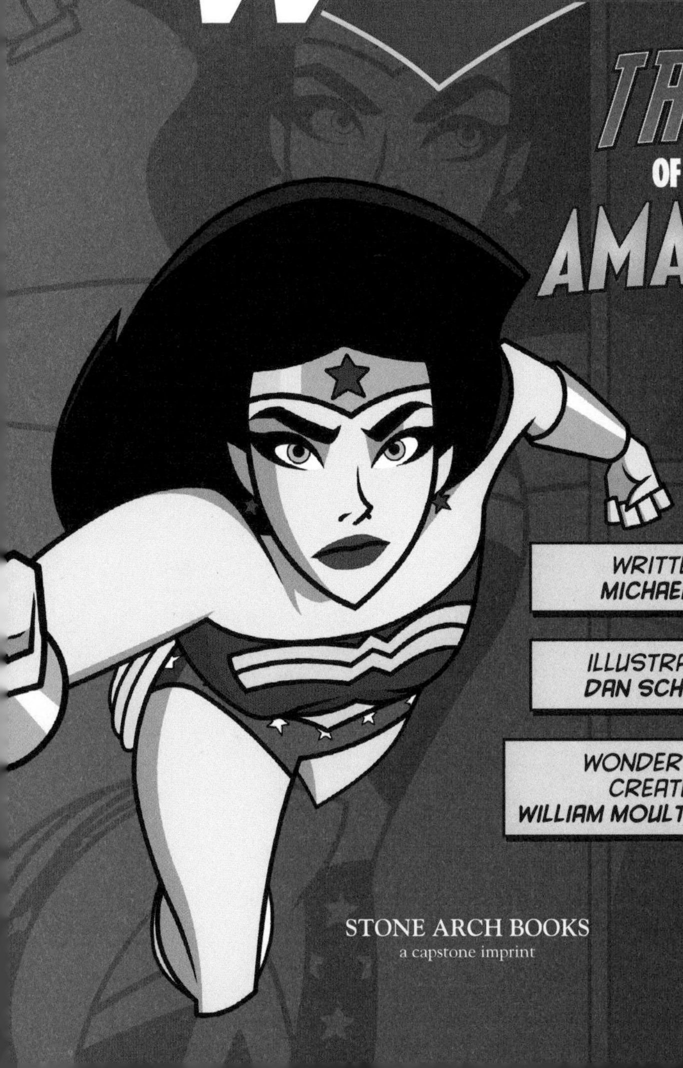

WRITTEN BY
MICHAEL DAHL

ILLUSTRATED BY
DAN SCHOENING

WONDER WOMAN
CREATED BY
WILLIAM MOULTON MARSTON

STONE ARCH BOOKS
a capstone imprint

Published by Stone Arch Books in 2010
A Capstone Imprint
151 Good Counsel Drive, P.O. Box 669
Mankato, Minnesota 56002
www.capstonepub.com

Library of Congress Cataloging-in-Publication Data

Dahl, Michael.
  Trial of the Amazons / by Michael Dahl ; illustrated by Dan Schoening.
    p. cm. -- (DC super heroes. Wonder Woman)
  ISBN 978-1-4342-1883-4 (library binding) -- ISBN 978-1-4342-2263-3
(pbk.)
  [1. Superheroes--Fiction. 2. Amazons--Fiction.] I. Schoening, Dan, ill. II.
Title.
  PZ7.D15134Tr 2010
  [Fic]--dc22   2009029096

Summary: When a fighter jet crashes on Paradise Island, young Princess
Diana asks her mother, Queen Hippolyta, for permission to enter the
world of mortals. The queen holds a special competition, a test of skill
and bravery, to determine which Amazonian will be permitted to go. But
Diana, as a royal princess, is denied from entering the trials! Against her
mother's wishes, the princess dons a mask and sets out to prove the she is
indeed the best of them — that she alone is a Wonder Woman.

Art Director: Bob Lentz
Designer: Emily Harris
Production Specialist: Michelle Biedscheid

Printed in the United States of America in Stevens Point, Wisconsin.
092009
005619WZS10

TABLE OF CONTENTS

CHAPTER 1

A DANGEROUS DIVE

"Don't jump, Diana! It's too dangerous!"

A handful of young women stood on a windy cliff on the island of Themyscira. A hundred feet below, ocean waves pounded and swirled. One woman, Clea, stared down at the foaming waves and shuddered.

"There are rocks down there," added Clea. "I don't think you should do this, Diana. We all know you're the best diver."

Clea was speaking to another young woman, who was kneeling on the ground.

While lacing up her sandals, Diana stared up at her friend. "You may think I'm the best, Clea," she said, "but I still have to prove it to myself."

"What will your mother, the queen, say?" Cleo asked.

Diana stood up and shrugged. "What she always says. 'Dignity, Diana. Remember your dignity.'" A few of the other women giggled. Clea frowned.

"Well, you *are* the princess of the Amazons," Clea said.

"Right," said Diana. "Which reminds me." She pulled her crown from her dark, waving hair and handed it to her friend. "Hold this for me."

Diana threw a glance at the churning waves below her.

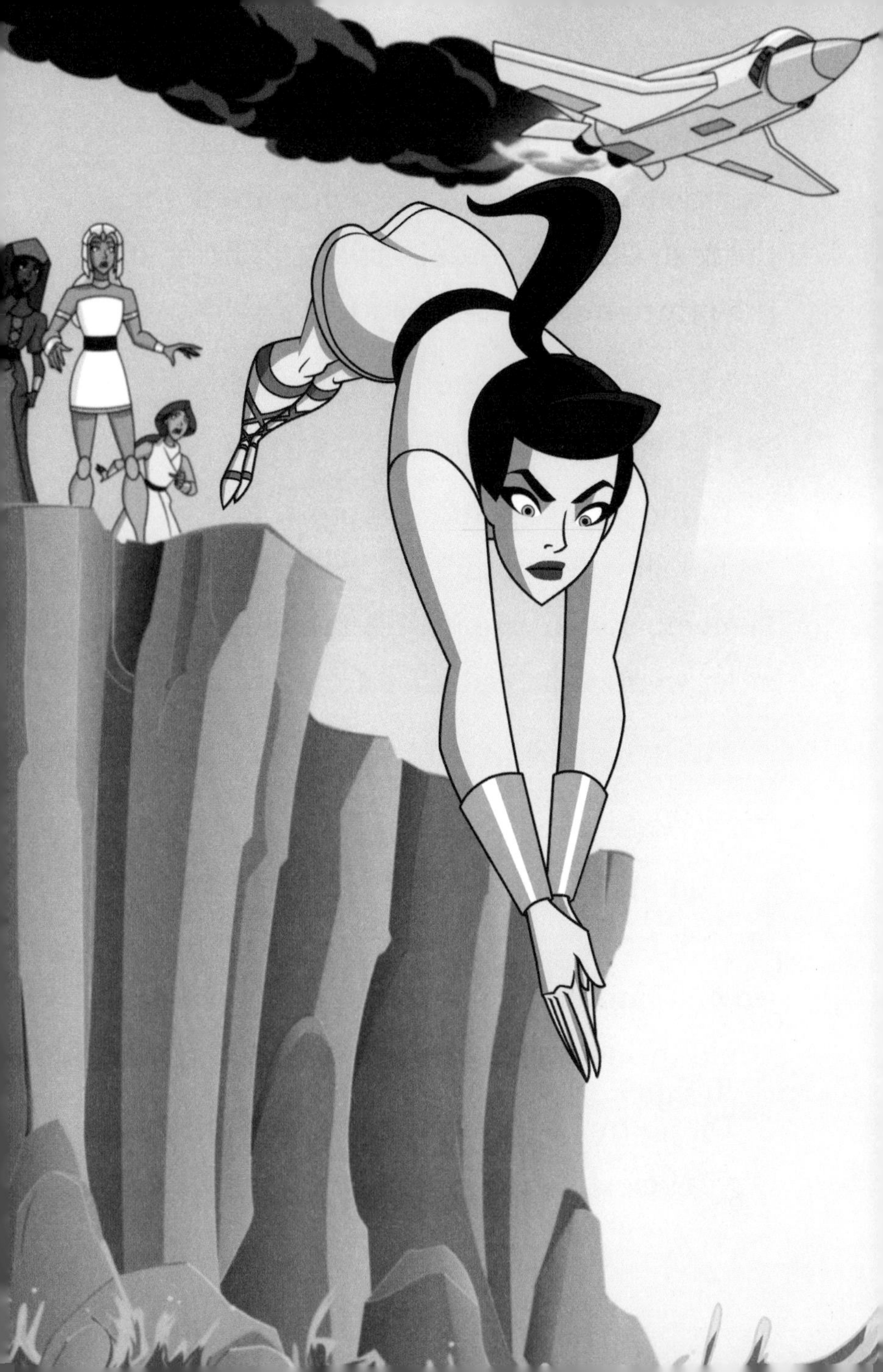

She took a deep breath, relaxed her shoulders, and then leaped off the cliff. Her hands and arms formed a sharp V-shape. The princess dived headfirst toward the water like an arrow.

SPLASH! Seconds later, Diana's head burst above the surface of the ocean. She gulped in deep lungfuls of air. She had done it! Then she looked up at her friends on the edge of the cliff. Diana waved and smiled. But her companions were not looking at her.

High in the cloudless blue sky, a fighter jet streamed above the island. As Diana watched, the nose of the jet dipped dangerously toward the ocean.

"It's going to crash!" Diana shouted.

The jet crashed into the water. Without thinking, the Amazon princess swam toward the impact. Her powerful arms carried her smoothly through the waves.

SPLASH! Something hit the water nearby. Diana turned and saw a parachute landing on the ocean. Strapped to the parachute's harness was a pilot in a military flight suit. The young man seemed to be unconscious.

The princess swam quickly to the man's side. She hooked one arm around his neck and then turned back to shore, pulling his motionless body through the waves. She headed toward a section of the island with a gravel beach.

The young man needed medical attention, but Diana knew that bringing the man onto the island was impossible.

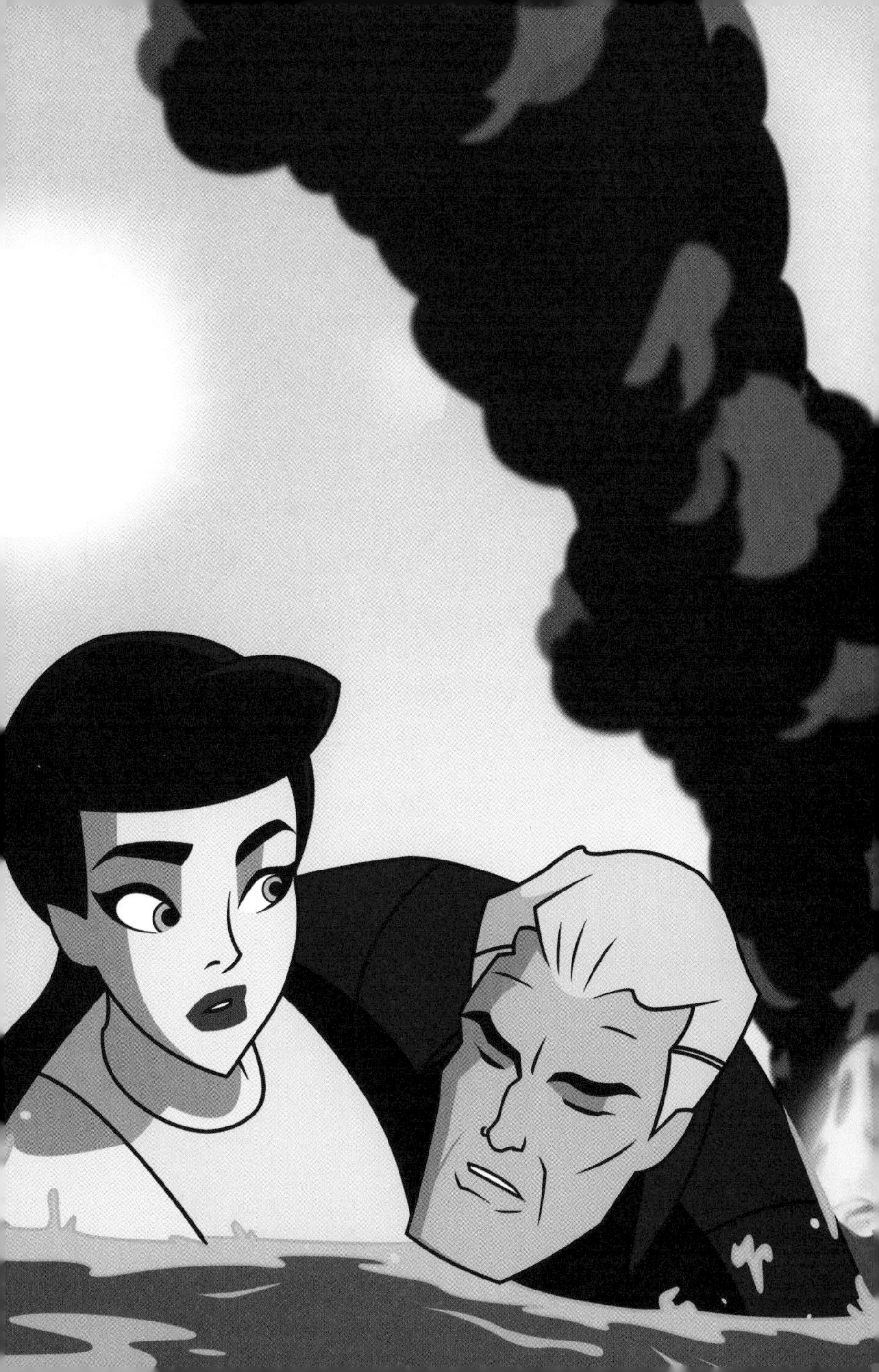

According to ancient law, no man could set foot on the island of Themyscira. Since the beginning of time, only Amazons, the female warriors, were allowed to live there. All male trespassers were put to death.

According to the same law, the day a man set foot on Themiscyra was the day the island would sink into the ocean. The Amazons would disappear forever.

Diana, however, was determined to save the injured pilot. Her brain was as strong as her muscles. The princess would figure out a way to help him.

CHAPTER 2

THE GOD OF WAR

Hippolyta, the queen of the Amazons, was furious. She was staring into her magical orb that rested in a hidden chamber deep within the royal palace. The orb had the power to show the queen any scene from the world of humans. Today, what the queen saw made her angry and frightened.

Hippolyta strode from the chamber and summoned one of her servants. "Send for the princess," ordered the queen.

"She is already here," said the servant.

"Diana is waiting for you in the meeting hall. And she has . . . " The servant turned red with shame.

"What is it?" the queen asked.

Hippolyta thought the young servant was going to faint. Swiftly, the ruler of the Amazons marched to the royal hall.

As soon as Hippolyta entered the room, she froze with disbelief. In the center of the room stood her daughter, Diana — proud, athletic, and still a little wet. Next to her stood four of the girl's companions. The friends held a crude hammock, woven of reeds and grass. Lying on the hammock was the body of an unconscious mortal from the outside world. A man.

Hippolyta's eyes blazed. "Have you lost your mind?" cried the queen.

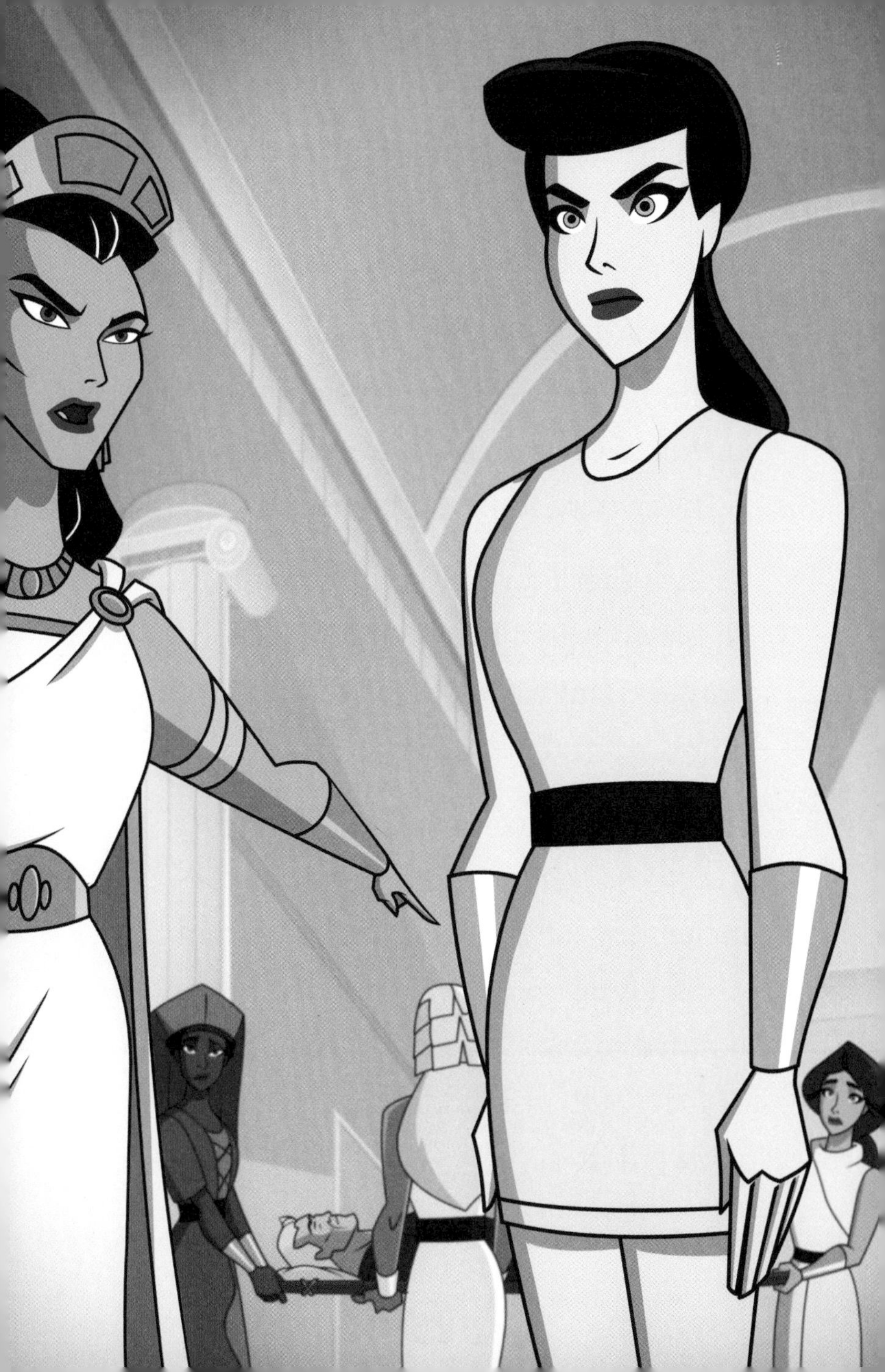

"How can you bring this man onto our island? You will bring the destruction of our world!" shouted the queen.

Diana dropped to one knee. "Listen, mother," she said. "Do you hear the earthquakes rumbling? Are the mountains of Themyscira falling into the sea?"

The other four girls trembled with fear. Hippolyta raised her head and listened. The marble chamber was silent except for the breathing of the sleeping man.

"You don't hear anything, because it isn't happening," said Diana. "The ancient law of the Amazons states that no man may *set foot* on Themyscira." Diana gestured to the hammock. "Well, he hasn't set foot on the island. In fact, he hasn't *touched* it at all."

Queen Hippolyta grinned at her daughter's cleverness. "You still haven't explained why you brought this mortal here," she said.

"His plane fell into the sea," said Diana. "I couldn't let him die. It is the duty of the Amazons to protect and defend the helpless, no matter who they are."

"I am well aware of the duty of the Amazons," said Hippolyta. "I am also aware that the duty of the Princess of the Amazons is to protect her sisters from the outside world."

The queen frowned. "Take him to the infirmary," she said. "Have his wounds tended. I will decide his fate later."

Queen Hippolyta turned to her daughter. "Come with me, Diana."

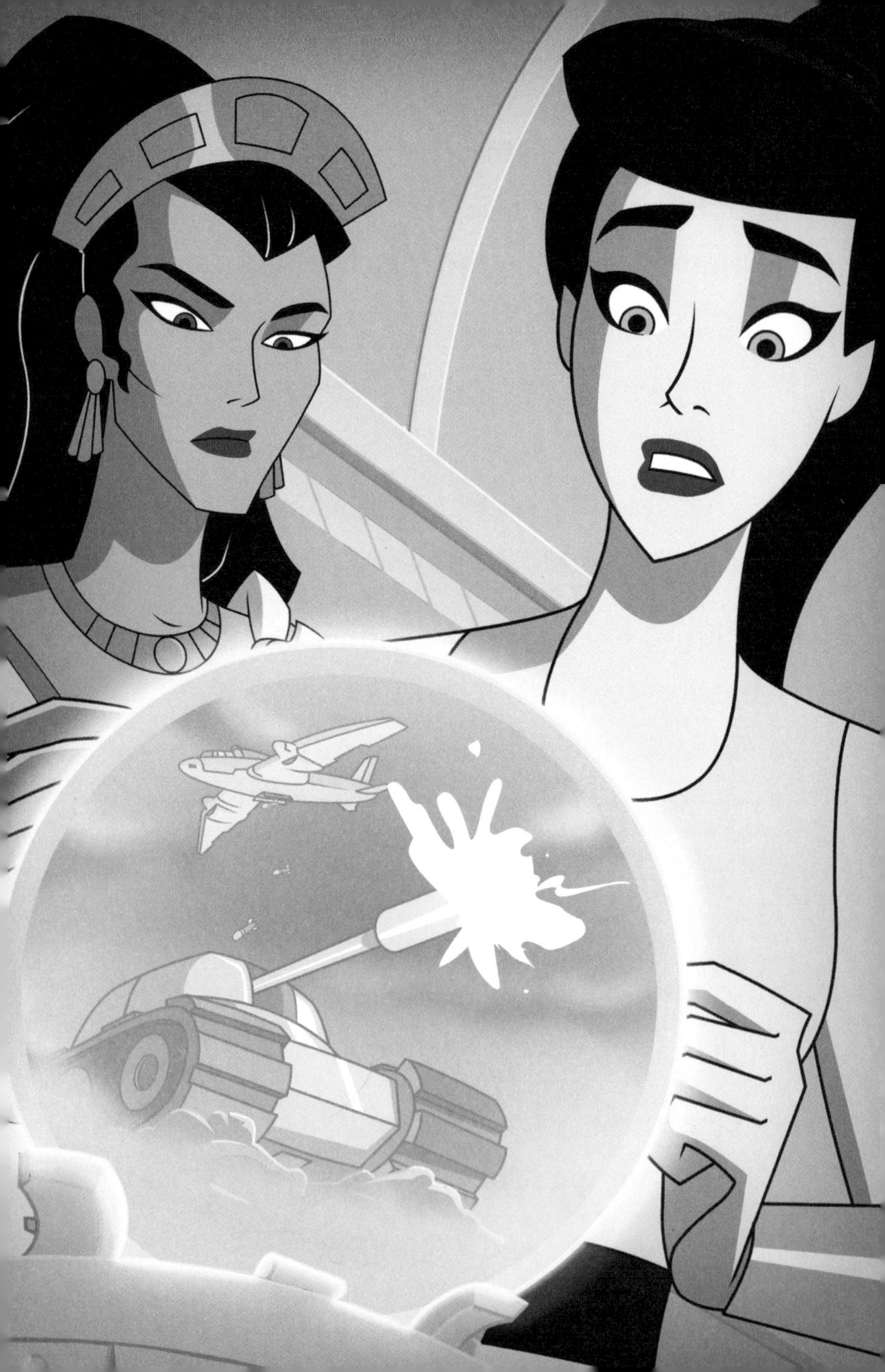

Within the queen's hidden chamber, she beckoned Diana to look into the magical orb. Diana's eyes grew wide with horror.

BOOM! FLASH! Bombs exploded. Buildings collapsed. People screamed. The orb showed scene after scene of death and destruction. Starvation, famine, and bloodshed ravaged the world of mortals. Each scene was worse than the last. Diana turned away, filled with pity and horror.

"This is why we retreated from mortals," said the queen. "The world has always been a place of greed and cruelty. But now, it has grown worse. Ares, the God of War, is gaining strength. His invisible servants stir up fear and confusion."

"We must defeat this evil before it reaches us," said Diana. "We must send one of our best Amazons to battle Ares."

"We must send a champion, trained on the battlefield of immortals," Diana added. "We must send someone who knows the power of the gods. Someone who can lead the mortals to peace and harmony."

Diana took a deep breath. "We must send one of our own," said Diana. "I will go."

The queen's expression turned grim. "You?" she cried in disbelief.

"I am the best," said Diana. "I am the strongest and most skilled of our warriors."

Queen Hippolyta sighed. "I know it, Diana, but you are also a princess. You were born to rule. You cannot leave Themyscira without an heir to our throne."

"May you rule for a thousand years," said Diana.

"Meanwhile," the princess added, "let me help the mortals while I can."

The queen left the chamber and walked rapidly to a balcony that overlooked the city of the Amazons. Diana followed.

"We *will* send a champion," said Hippolyta, pointing outside. "The champion will come from our sisters out there — not from inside this household."

"But —" Diana began.

Hippolyta raised a hand.

"Warriors are many," the queen said. "Princesses are few. We shall find our champion according to the ancient laws. We shall have a contest. The Trial of the Amazons."

CHAPTER 3

THE MASK OF BRONZE

One week after Queen Hippolyta's decision, a field in the center of the island had been cleared, smoothed, and filled with wooden stands. A vast crowd sat in the stands. They watched as the queen entered the field in a chariot drawn by white stallions.

"Hail Hippolyta! Hail to our queen!" the crowd chanted.

The queen reined in her horses and waved to the crowd. "Today, we choose one of our own," she said.

"Today, we choose our best warrior," Hippolyta announced. "After a day of contests and events, only one warrior will remain. And that warrior shall represent all Amazons as she fights the power of evil in the world of mortals."

Hippolyta raised her arms to the sky. "So now," she commanded, "let the Trial of the Amazons begin!"

Trumpets sounded. Voices cheered. A parade of one hundred contestants marched onto the grassy field. The women were armed with javelins and shields. Some of them wore helmets and armbands. And one, standing apart from the rest, wore a strange bronze mask that shielded her face. The mask gleamed in the sunlight.

All the warriors bowed toward the queen as she took her seat in the stands.

Then the Trial began.

The first event was called Arrows and Rings. This challenge tested a warrior's skill and concentration. A small device tossed nine metal rings into the air. Each warrior had to shoot an arrow at the rings.

The rings were each tightly covered with cloth like the skin of a drum. The warriors whose arrows pierced the cloth and captured the most rings would move on to the next event.

Bows hummed and arrows soared. Several warriors captured three or four rings at a time.

Then, the warrior in the brass helmet took her turn. Carefully, she drew back the string of her bow. Rings were released into the air.

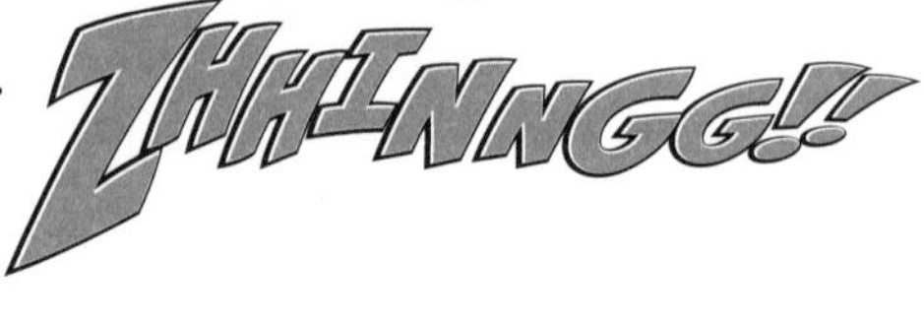
ZHHINNGG!!

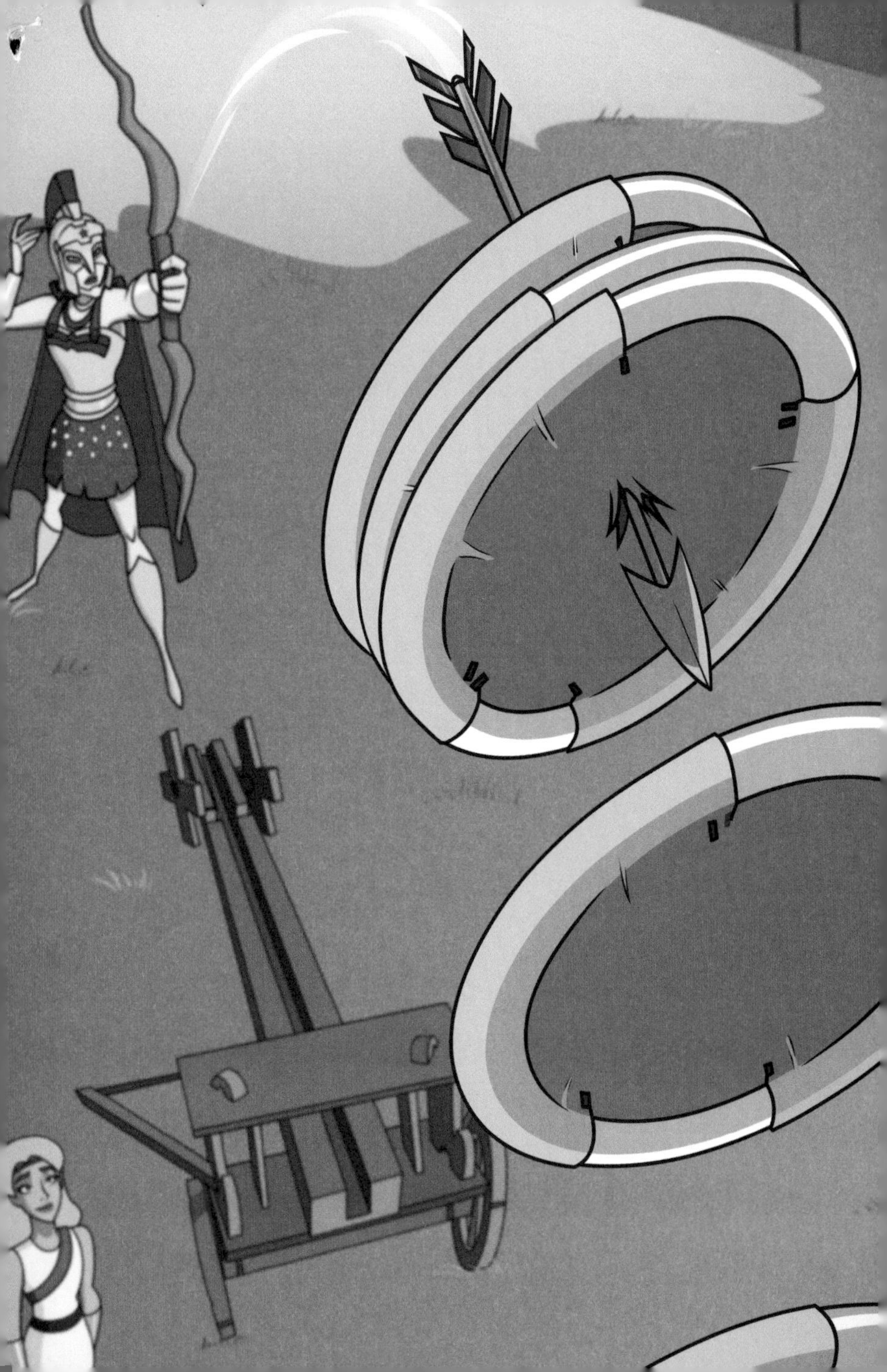

Schinggggg! The masked warrior's arrow flashed toward the nine rings. When the arrow landed in the grass, a young girl ran and fetched it. She lifted the arrow above her head. It had captured all nine rings. The audience cheered loudly for the mysterious victor.

An elderly councilor next to the queen leaned forward. "Where is Princess Diana?" she asked. "Is she coming to watch?"

Hippolyta frowned. She knew that Diana was upset. The queen glanced toward the palace. On the balcony stood a familiar figure with long black hair and a crown.

"The princess has chosen to watch from the palace," answered the queen. She did not mention that her daughter was too angry to join her in the stands.

All morning the Trial continued. The next events were the Obstacle Race, the Javelin Throw, and the Deer Chase. After a break at noon, each warrior had to recite a poem about famous battles and Amazon heroes. The band of contestants that moved on to each new event grew smaller and smaller, but the masked warrior was always included in the winning group.

As evening approached, only two warriors remained — the masked warrior and the mighty Themis. Queen Hippolyta approached them.

"You have done well," said the queen. "Only one test remains. This test shall require all of your strength and courage."

Low hills bordered the edge of the grassy field. The queen led the two warriors toward one of the hills.

The mouth of a dark cave loomed in front of them. Hippolyta pointed toward the entrance. "No one shall watch this trial," she said. "Not even me. For this is the Cave of Truth. Whatever test the gods have devised for you within, only the best warrior shall step forth as the winner. Go, my sisters, and may Hera help you!"

The two young women bowed to the queen. Then they disappeared into the mysterious tunnel.

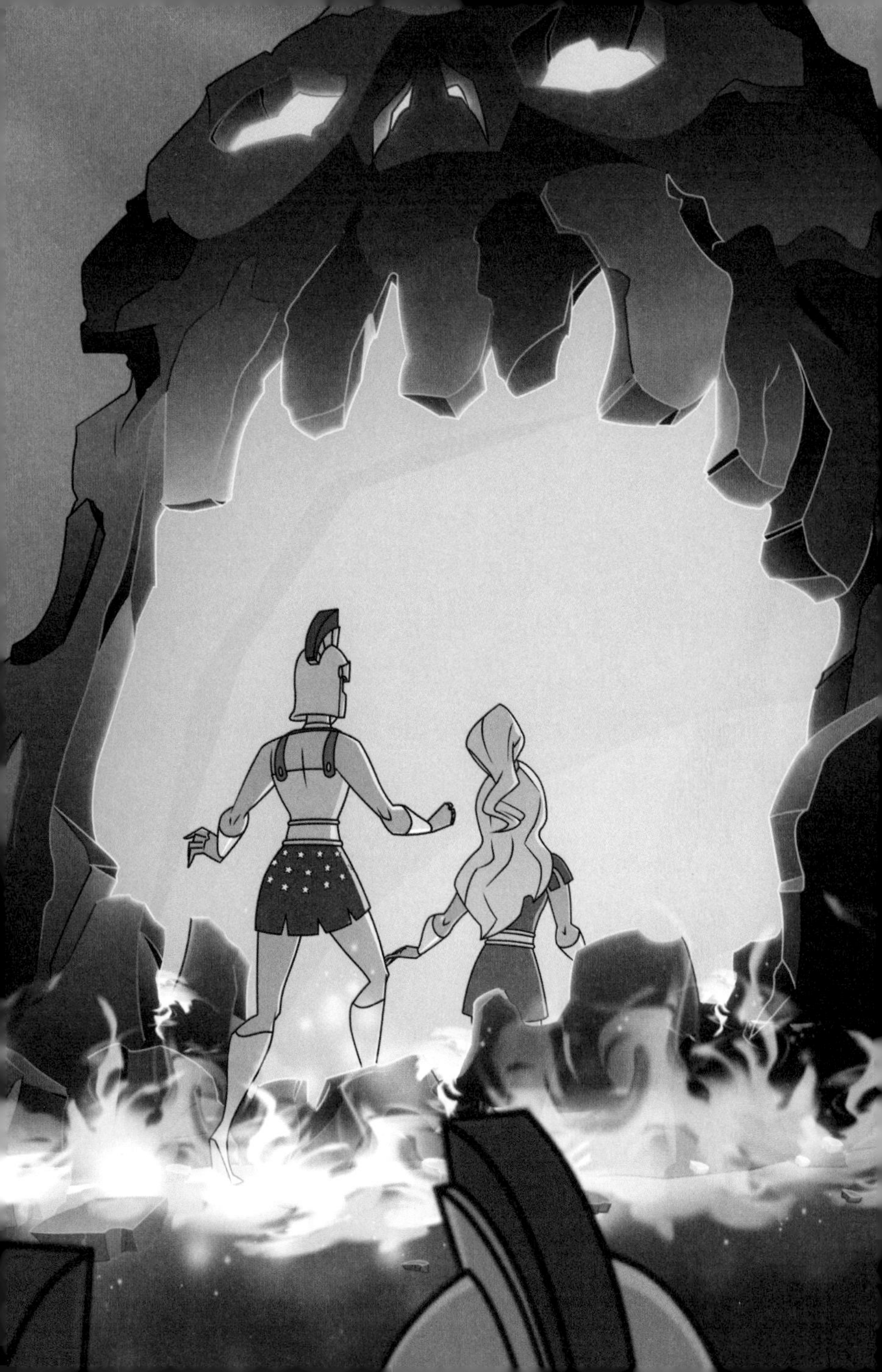

CHAPTER 4

THE CAVE OF TRUTH

Soon, the tunnel became as black as a moonless night. The two women slowly moved forward. They felt along the rough sides of the cave to guide themselves. Their eyes were useless in the thick gloom.

After what seemed like hours, the shadows lifted. The warriors saw a flickering light at the end of the rocky passage.

"Themis," said the Masked Warrior. "Stop."

Themis frowned. "Why? Are you afraid, sister?" she demanded.

The masked warrior bowed her head. "This is the Cave of Truth," she said. "There can be no secrets here." She removed the brass helmet and mask from her head.

"Diana!" cried Themis.

The princess of the Amazons stood unveiled before her friend. "Yes, it is I," said Diana. "I could not continue the Trial without telling you."

"Does the queen know?" asked Themis.

Diana shook her head. "My mother doesn't wish me to compete," she said. "But I had to follow my heart."

RUMMMMMMBLE! The cave trembled. The warriors staggered on the rocky floor. A giant shadow rose up to meet them.

POOF! Fires suddenly blazed from the walls of the cave. The light revealed a warrior standing before them. He stood twenty feet tall and was made of gray rock. He gripped a giant spear and shield.

"Whose statue is that?" asked Themis.

Diana saw the figure of an hourglass carved into the shield. "That is no statue," she said.

The stony figure opened its eyes. They gleamed like fiery comets.

"I am Chronos," said the warrior.

Diana shuddered. Chronos was the god of time. He was the father of *all* the gods.

"I watched your Trial, young Amazons," said Chronos. "Queen Hippolyta has tested your skill and strength. It is *I*, however, who will challenge your spirit."

KRAK! Chronos pounded the end of his spear against the cave floor.

"Behold the Chasm of Chronos!" boomed the god.

A crack appeared in the rock beneath the god's spear. The crack zigzagged along the ground, growing wider and deeper. A stream of water flowed through the crack, and soon it became a deep river.

"As the chasm winds through the tunnels, it grows wider and more dangerous," said Chronos. "Your test is to leap across the crack, one at a time. You shall keep jumping, back and forth, following the river downstream. Each time you will be forced to jump farther. Eventually, one of you shall fail. The warrior whose feet lands at the farthest point shall become the winner."

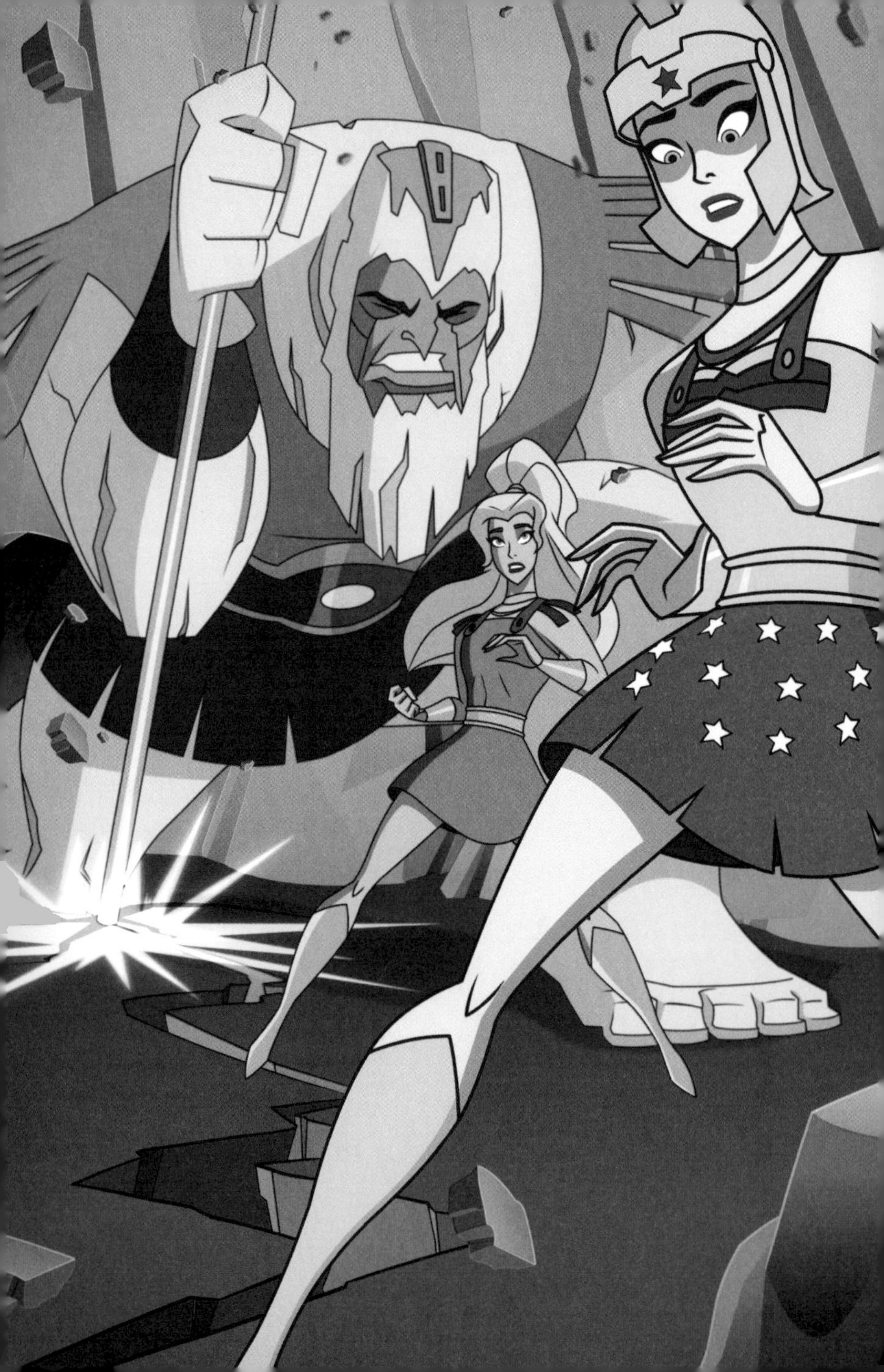

Themis and Diana both eyed the widening chasm.

"There is more," said Chronos. "This is the Cave of Truth. To discover the truth of your courage, I have removed your immortality. You are now like the humans of the outer world. You can feel pain. You can be wounded. You can even be killed."

"My mother did not warn us of this," said Diana.

"Hippolyta does not know," said Chronos. "She asked only for a test from the gods, and I shall give you such a test."

The god turned his flaming eyes on the women. Princess Diana heard a voice deep within her head. It sounded like the hiss of a snake. "Hippolyta does not know that her own daughter may lose her life."

"When do we begin, Chronos?" Diana asked.

The stony giant dissolved into the shadows. "Follow the river," whispered Chronos. "It shall lead you out of the cave. Beware — it may also lead to death."

The two warriors moved forward. The chasm was only a few feet wide at first. It was easy to leap across. The farther they moved downstream, the wider the chasm grew. Soon, Diana had to take a running start before she jumped.

At one point, Themis's sandal caught on the edge of the chasm. She quickly regained her balance.

Diana leaped and heard the rush of the deep river flowing below her. She, too, reached the other side.

Finally, the two warriors came to a point where the chasm was thirty feet wide. On the other side was a tunnel that led outside. "This is our final jump," said Themis. "May Hera give me strength!"

Themis stepped back several yards from the edge of the chasm, then she ran as quickly as she could. At the edge, she pushed off with her powerful legs.

WHOOOOSH!

Up she soared. Themis raised her arms and aimed toward the other side.

Oomf! Themis fell onto the face of the opposite cliff. Her fingers fought to find a hold on the rock. She dangled helplessly above the river.

"Don't jump, Diana! It's too dangerous!" Themis cried out.

"I'm coming over to help you," said Diana.

Like Themis, Diana stepped back several paces from the edge of the chasm. The Princess of the Amazons took a deep breath. She relaxed her shoulders. Then, she ran and leaped off the cliff.

She sailed through the air. Her bare feet would have easily reached the other side, but that was not their goal. Instead, Diana landed next to Themis on the edge. **THUD!**

Diana used her free arm to push Themis up toward the lip of the chasm. "Grab the edge!" she yelled.

Using her last shred of strength, Themis pulled herself up onto the edge. Then she reached down toward Diana. She pulled her friend up beside her.

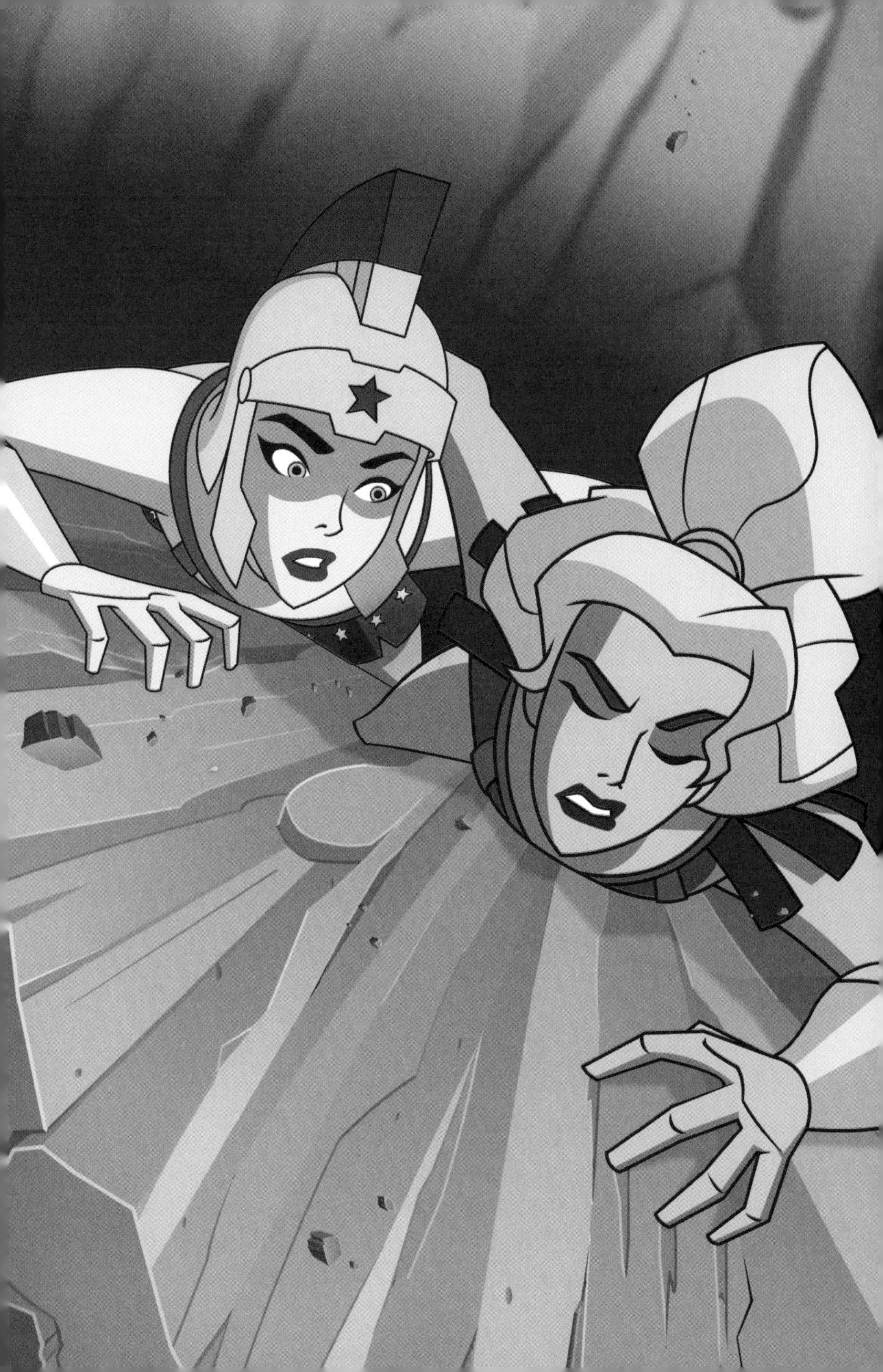

Diana breathed heavily, kneeling on the rocky ground. She turned to her companion and said, "You have won, Themis. You reached the edge before I did."

"Only because your strength was greater than mine," said Themis.

Diana shook her head. "The Cave of Truth does not ask for excuses. According to the rules of the test, you have won."

Themis rose to her feet. She dusted herself off, lifted her head, and walked out of the cave. For a long while, Diana did not move. She sat at the edge of the cliff and gazed down at the dark river. She thought of the trick she had played on her mother.

"Chronos was right," Diana said to herself. "A true warrior must not hide. She must be herself and face the consequences."

Then, Diana stood up. She unbound her hair and let it fall to her shoulders. Her helmet had been left far behind. *No matter,* thought Diana. She would not need it now.

She walked out of the cave, ready to face the anger of her royal mother.

CHAPTER 5

WONDER WOMAN

As Diana walked into the sunlight, she heard the crowds cheering for Themis. Themis would now become the champion of the Amazons. She would travel to the outside world and fight side by side with humans. She would use her amazing abilities to defeat the evil power of Ares.

Themis ran to Diana's side and grabbed her hand. A wide smile brightened Themis's face.

"They are cheering for *you*, Diana," Themis said.

"I don't understand," said the princess.

Suddenly, the cheering stopped. Silence fell over the grassy field. Queen Hippolyta was riding her chariot straight toward Diana.

The majestic stallions pawed at the air and stopped a few steps from Diana's bare feet. Hippolyta rushed out of the chariot and onto the ground.

"What is the meaning of this deception?" she thundered.

Diana kneeled and lowered her head. "Forgive me, Mother," she said, "but how could I send one of my sisters into the world to battle if I am not willing to fight, too?"

Hippolyta stretched out her hand and helped her daughter to her feet. "Spoken like a true princess," she said.

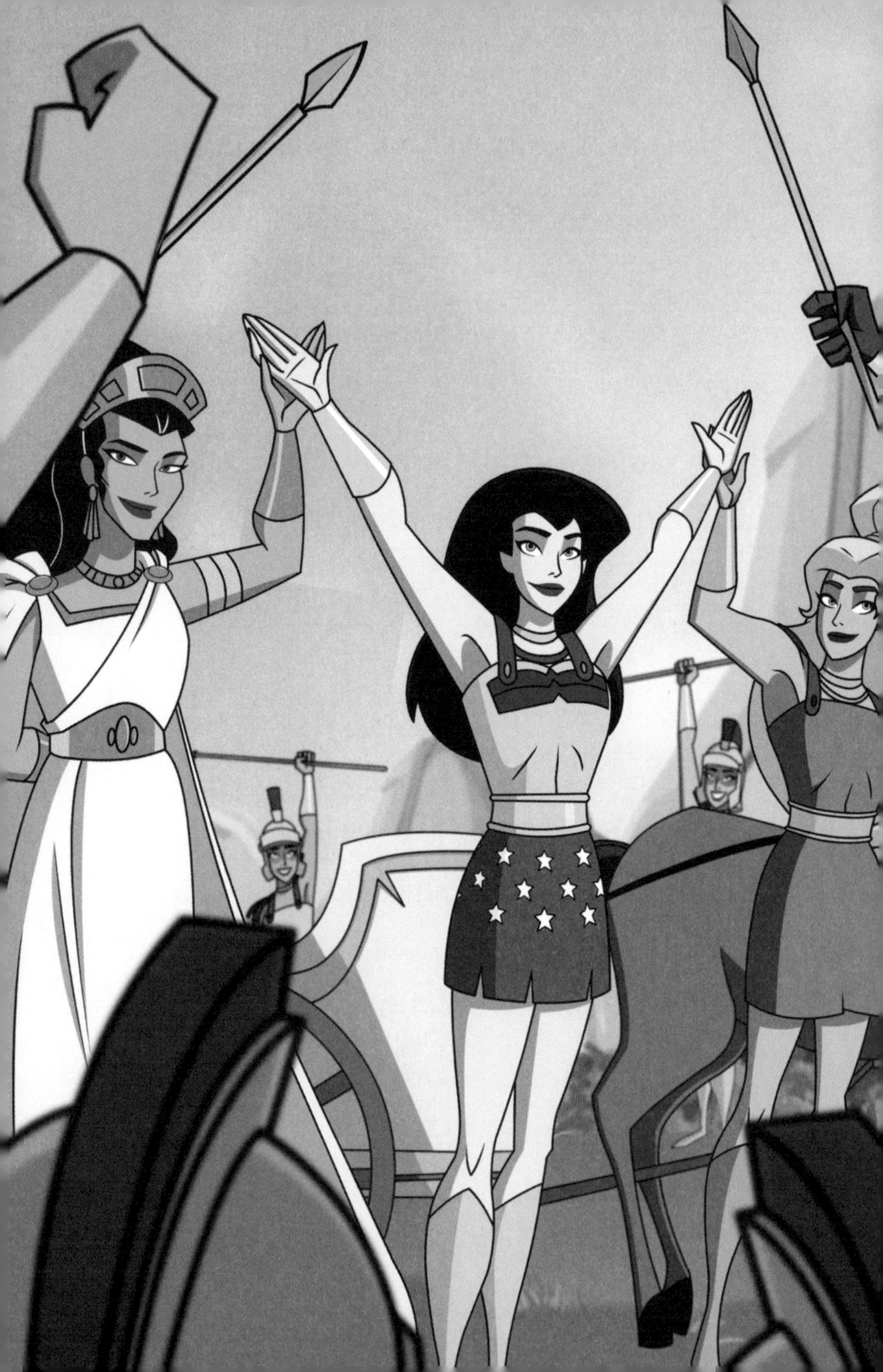

The queen led her daughter into the chariot. She snapped a whip and the horses snorted. They raced back toward the stands that held the onlooking Amazons.

Hippolyta addressed the crowd. "Themis the Bold has told us what happened in the Cave of Truth. She has told us how another warrior saved her life. A warrior who showed not only bravery and strength, but also the other qualities of a true Amazon: kindness, fairness, and self-sacrifice.

"That warrior has won the Trial of the Amazons," continued the queen. "And that warrior is my daughter – Princess Diana."

ROOAAAARRR!! The Amazons in the stands cheered with joy.

"You're not angry with me?" whispered Diana.

"No. I'm proud of you, my daughter," said Hippolyta, smiling.

Three young women dressed in gold ran from the stands. They each held a precious object that they handed to the queen.

"These gifts shall help you in your battles," said Hippolyta. "First, is the Golden Lasso. A person trapped in its coils is forced to tell the truth."

Next, the queen gave Diana a new pair of silver bracelets. "These have been forged by the weapon-maker of the gods. They will defend you and those who seek your protection."

The third servant handed the queen a shining band of gold.

"Take this golden tiara," said Queen Hippolyta.

"It can fly through the air, cut through steel and stone, and will serve as a symbol of your royalty," the queen said.

Dignity, thought Diana. *Always dignity.*

"By the way, daughter, who was the young woman who watched the Trial from our balcony?" the queen asked. "The one who looked like you?"

Diana coughed. "Um, that was my friend Clea. I'm sorry for deceiving you, Mother."

"I was surprised by your trick," said Queen Hippolyta, grinning. "This way, daughter. Now it is my turn to surprise you."

The Amazon champion followed her mother behind the wooden stands. A strange sight met her eyes.

The young pilot she had rescued from the ocean was sitting on the beach.

"He's touching the ground!" exclaimed Diana.

Hippolyta folded her arms. "Look closer," she said.

Diana squinted and saw that the pilot was not resting on the island. He floated several inches above the sand.

"Behold!" said the queen. **POOF!** She waved her hands, and a jet airplane appeared in front of them. It seemed to be made of glass. The pilot was inside the translucent machine.

"I don't understand," said Diana.

"You need something fast and light and invisible to humans for transportation," the queen said.

"This airplane will help transport you across the countries of the outer world," Hippolyta said.

"It's perfect," said Diana, smiling.

"You'll need it — you start your mission today," the queen said.

"Today?!" gasped Diana.

"The power of Ares must be stopped," said the queen. "Today is the beginning of your new life, Diana, and you can begin by taking this poor man back to his home."

Diana embraced her mother. "Thank you," said the princess. "I shall return one day. I promise."

Queen Hippolyta stood before her daughter, and placed both of her hands on Diana's shoulders.

"You truly are the best warrior we have," said the queen. "You are strong, resourceful, smart, and brave. You will do us proud, my daughter. Go forth to defeat the power of hatred and war. And never forget that you are a champion, an Amazon — a wonder woman!"

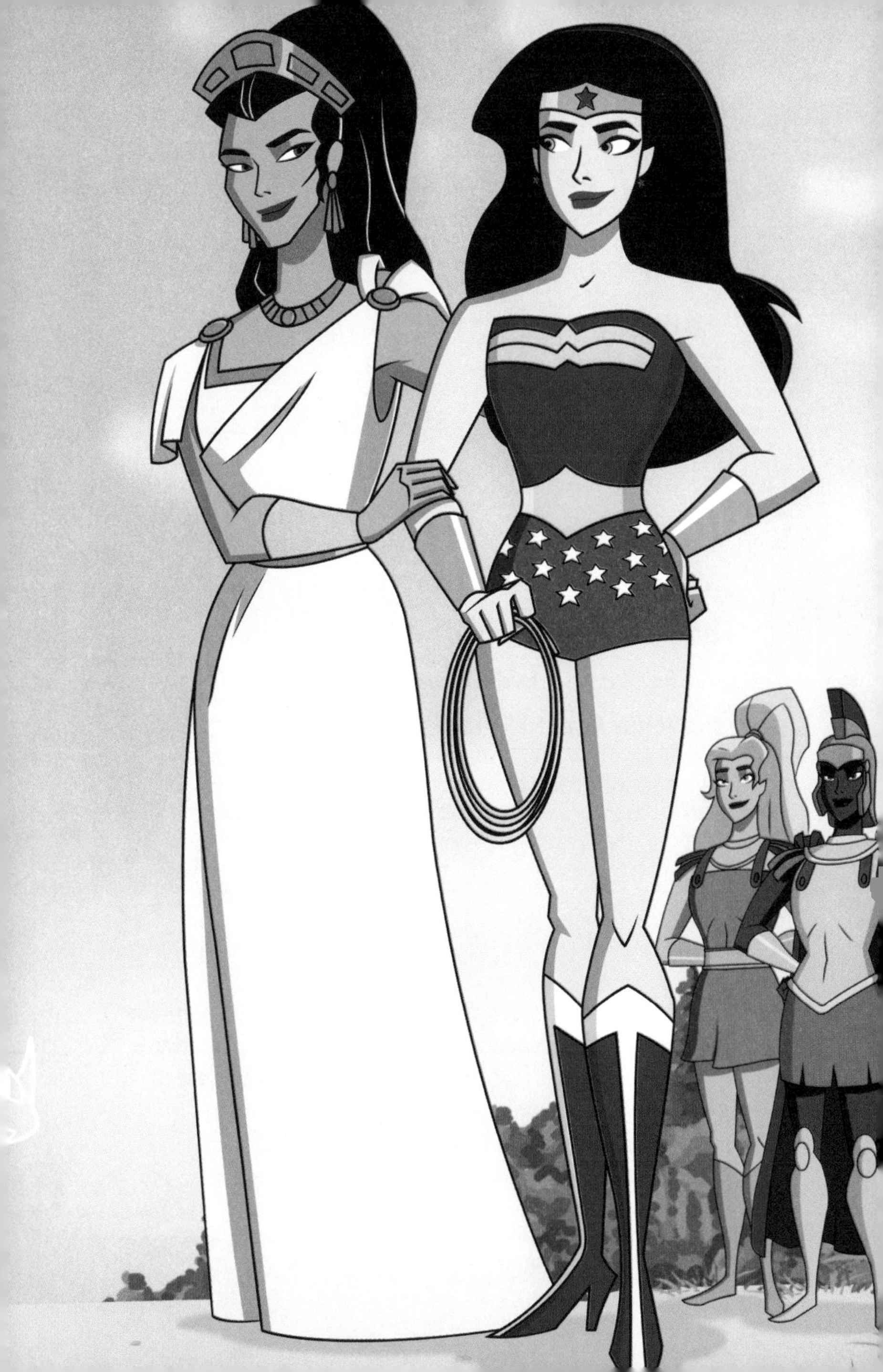

INVISIBLE PLANE
SECRET FILES

FILE NO. 3765 >>>QUEEN HIPPOLYTA

FRIEND » | ALLY | ENEMY

BIRTHPLACE: Themyscira

AGE: Unknown

HEIGHT: 5 ft 9 in **WEIGHT:** 150 lbs

EYES: Blue **HAIR:** Black

POWERS/ABILITIES: Immortality, super-strength, hand-to-hand combat skills, and leadership capabilities. Also, Hippolyta does not need to eat or drink as long as she remains on Themyscira.

BIOGRAPHY

Hippolyta is the current queen of the Amazons on the paradise island of Themyscira. She has been the ruler of the Amazons since the goddesses created the warrior race of women. Hippolyta is mother to Princess Diana, the current Wonder Woman. Hippolyta is also the founder of the paradise island of Themyscira, which is home and sanctuary to all of the Amazon warrior-women.

THE AMAZONS

The Amazon race was created from clay by five Greek goddesses. Hippolyta was the first Amazon created; therefore, the goddesses crowned her queen of all the Amazons. The second Amazon to come to life was Antiope. She was chosen as Hippolyta's second-in-command.

As a symbol of their roles as leaders, the goddesses gave Hippolyta and Antiope each a Golden Girdle. These girdles, or belts, enhanced their strength and abilities ten-fold, which made them fearsome and powerful leaders. As long as Hippolyta has her magic girdle, the Amazon race remains immortal on Themyscira Island.

POWERS

GIFTS FROM THE GODDESSES . . .

Each of the five goddesses gave Hippolyta and Antiope amazing gifts . . .

• Artemis, goddess of the hunt, gave them hunting and tracking skills.

• Athena, goddess of wisdom, gifted them with sharp, wise minds.

• Hestia, goddess of the hearth, built them warm, safe homes.

• Demeter, goddess of the harvest, ensured they would have plenty of food.

• The goddess of love, Aphrodite, made them beautiful — inside and out.

BIOGRAPHIES

Michael Dahl is the author of more than 200 books for children and young adults. He has won the AEP Distinguished Achievement Award three times for his non-fiction. His Finnegan Zwake mystery series was shortlisted twice by the Anthony and Agatha awards. He has also written the Library of Doom series and the Dragonblood books. He is a featured speaker at conferences around the country on graphic novels and high-interest books for boys.

Dan Schoening was born in Victoria, B.C. Canada. From an early age, Dan has had a passion for animation and comic books. Currently, Dan does freelance work in the animation and game industry, and spends a lot of time with his lovely little daughter, Paige.

GLOSSARY

beckoned (BEK-uhnd)—made a sign to someone, asking them to come closer

cruelty (KROO-uhl-tee)—causing pain to others on purpose

deception (di-SEP-shuhn)—a trick that makes people believe something is not true

determined (di-TUR-mind)—made a firm decision to do something

devised (di-VIZED)—thought something up, or invented something

dignity (DIG-nuh-tee)—a person who has dignity has a quality or manner that makes them worthy of respect

majestic (muh-JESS-tik)—having great power and beauty

recite (ri-SITE)—to say aloud something you have learned by heart

translucent (transs-LOO-suhnt)—something that is not completely clear like glass, but some light does get through

DISCUSSION QUESTIONS

1. Diana felt she was doing the right thing when she defied her mother's orders. When, if ever, is it okay to break the rules?

2. If you were Princess Diana, would you have risked victory to save Themis? Why or why not?

WRITING PROMPTS

1. Why do you think dignity is so important to Queen Hippolyta? Why is it important for a leader to act that way? Explain your answers.

2. If you had Diana's invisible jet plane, what would you do with it? Where would you go? Who would you see? Write about it.

3. Diana's mother, Queen Hippolyta, is very hard on her. Have your parents or guardians ever been hard on you? Do you think it was fair? Did anything good come from it? Write about what happened.

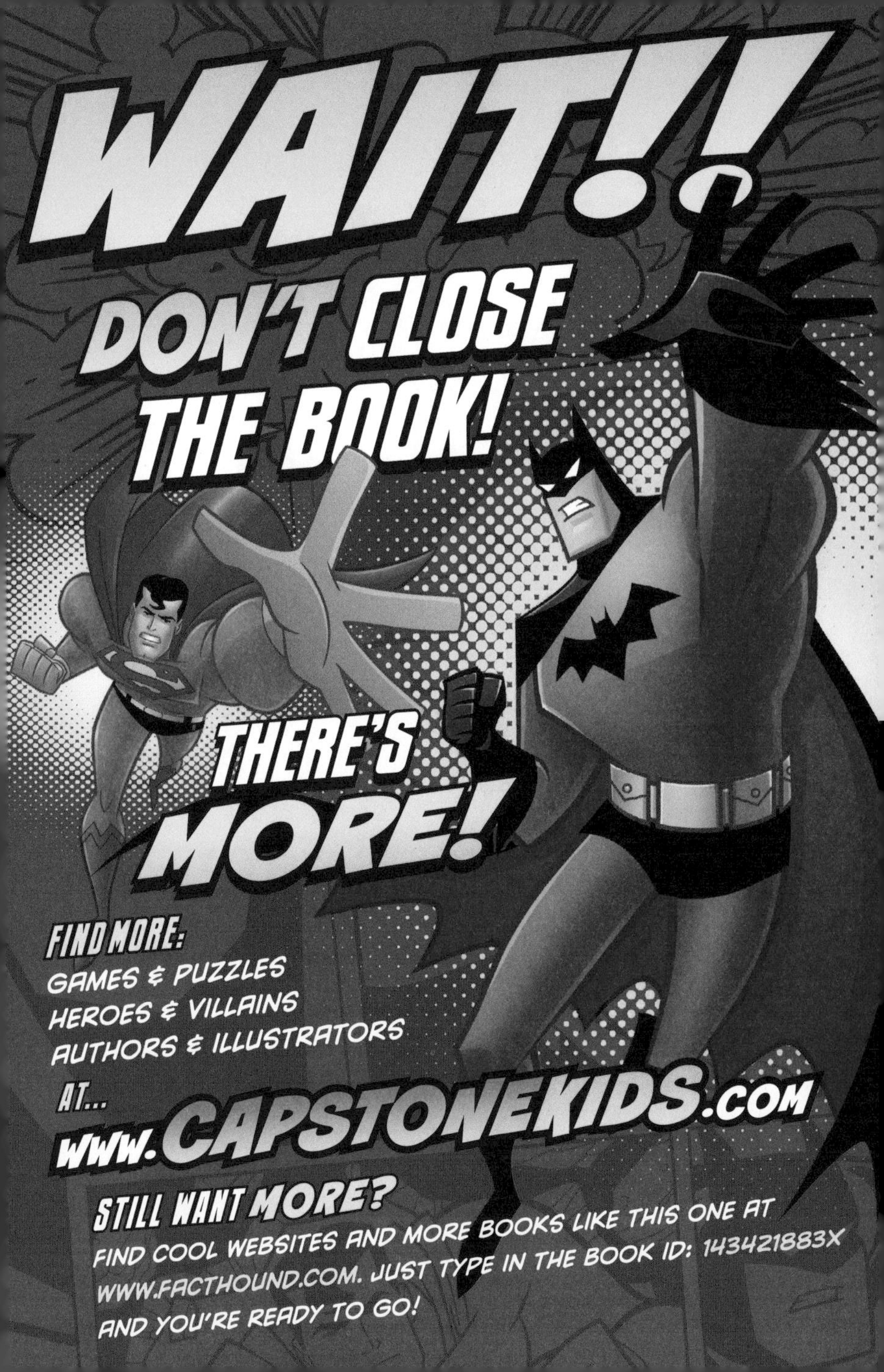
WAIT!!
DON'T CLOSE THE BOOK!
THERE'S MORE!
FIND MORE:
GAMES & PUZZLES
HEROES & VILLAINS
AUTHORS & ILLUSTRATORS
AT...
WWW.CAPSTONEKIDS.COM
STILL WANT MORE?
FIND COOL WEBSITES AND MORE BOOKS LIKE THIS ONE AT WWW.FACTHOUND.COM. JUST TYPE IN THE BOOK ID: 143421883X AND YOU'RE READY TO GO!

MORE NEW

WONDER WOMAN

ADVENTURES!

MONSTER MAGIC

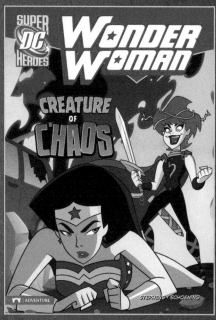

CREATURE OF CHAOS

ATTACK OF THE CHEETAH

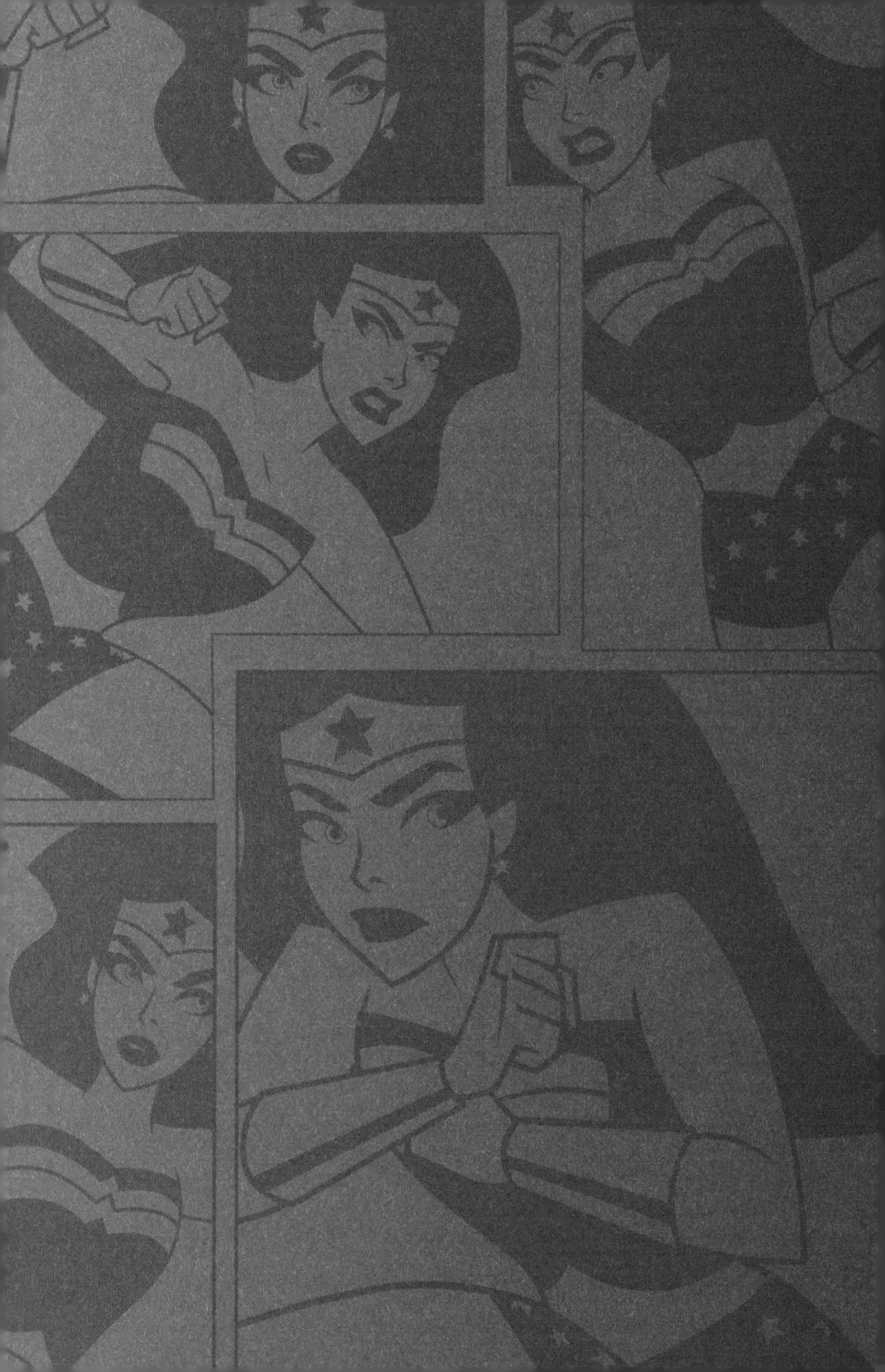

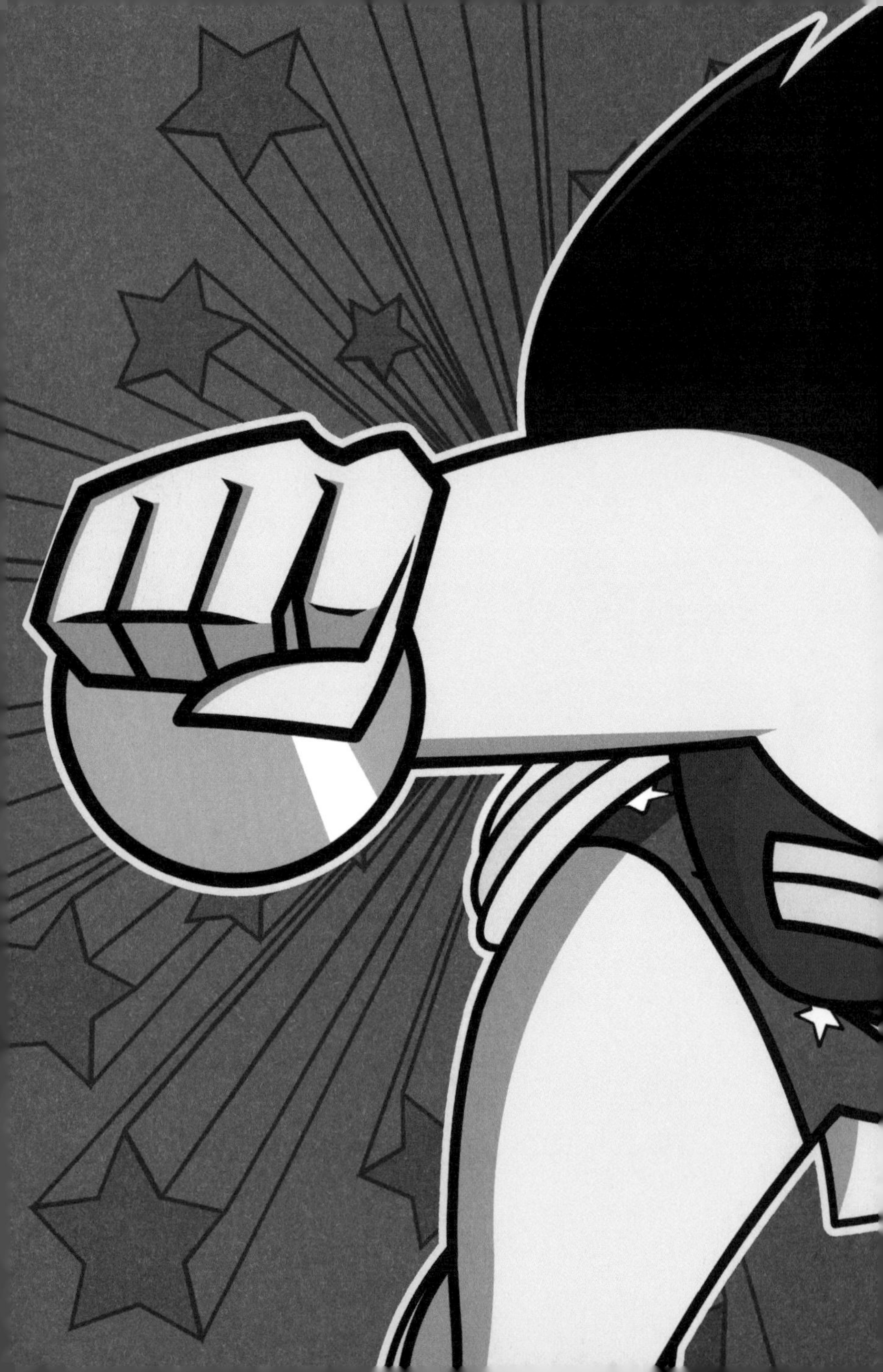

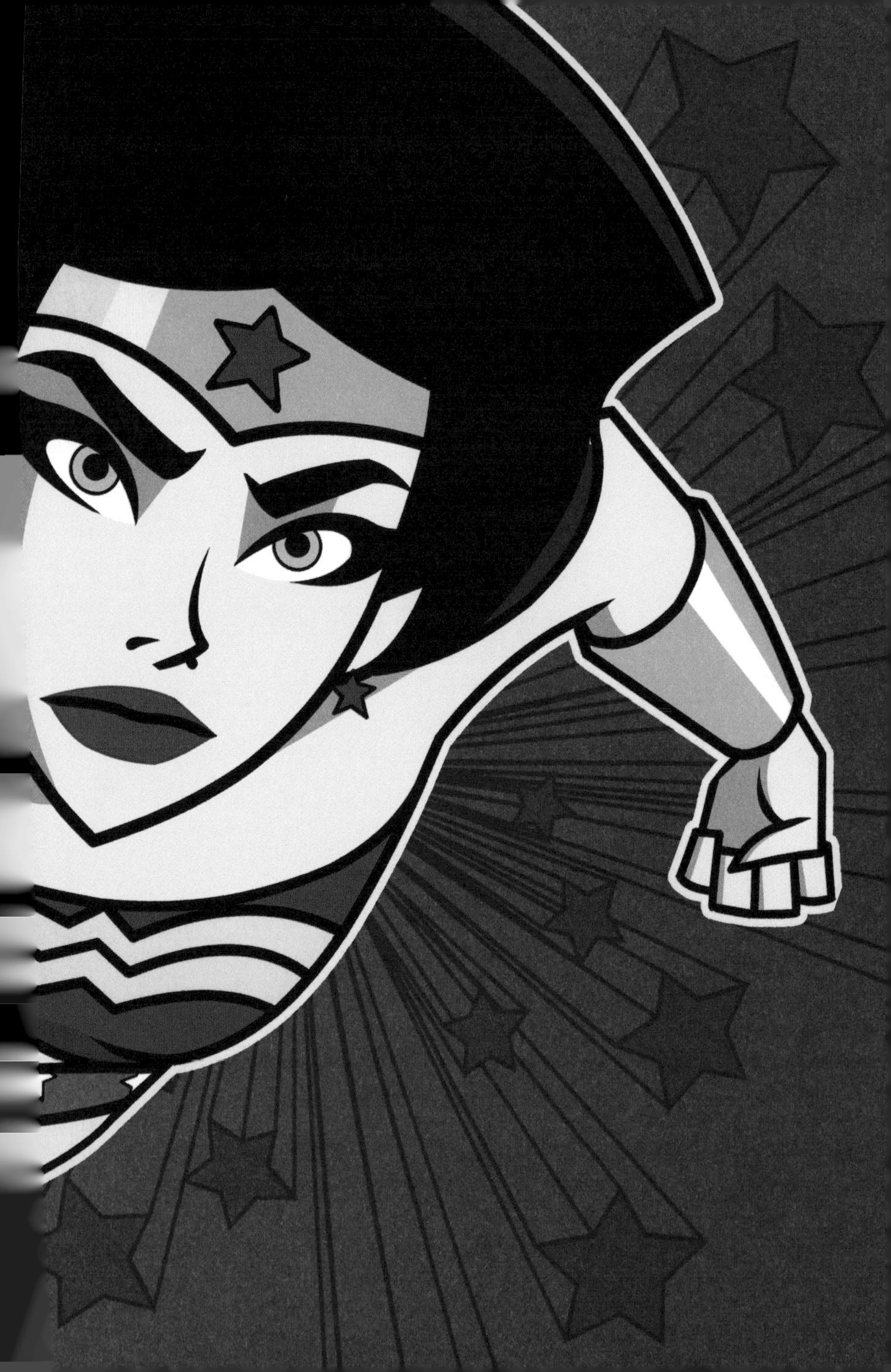